FRIENDS
OF ACPL

P9-CFX-845

Truffle's Christmas

First American edition 2000 published by Orchard Books

First published in Great Britain in 2000 by David Bennett Books

Orchard Books, A Grolier Company
95 Madison Avenue, New York, NY 10016

Manufactured in China
The text of this book is set in 24 point Adobe Garamond.
The illustrations are watercolor.

1 3 5 7 9 10 8 6 4 2

Library of Congress Cataloging-in-Publication Data
Currey, Anna.
Truffle's Christmas / by Anna Currey.—lst American ed.
p. cm.
Summary: Because of his unselfishness, a little mouse has his Christmas wishes fulfilled by Santa.
ISBN 0-531-30266-0 (trade)
[1. Mice—Fiction. 2. Christmas—Fiction. 3. Santa Claus—Fiction.] I. Title.
PZ7.C9345 Tr 2000 [E]—dc21 99-57950

Truffle's Christmas

by

Anna Currey

ORCHARD BOOKS / NEW YORK

Christmas was coming.
All the little mice had finished their letters to Santa—

all, that is, except for
Truffle. He couldn't
decide what he wanted.

“I’d really love a hula hoop . . .

but I wish we had a blanket, a nice new blanket without any holes. Then again . . .”

"You'll have to decide," said Emmeline, his big sister, who always knew best, "or Santa won't bring you anything. Here, you'd better start."

"Oh all right, a hula hoop then," said Truffle, throwing away his letter.

He put his new letter into an envelope and addressed it to "SANTER CLAWS, NORF POL."

On Christmas Eve the mice hung their stockings up in a neat row.

"I'm getting a nurse's uniform," announced Emmeline.
"I'm getting a chemistry set," said George, Truffle's big brother.
The littlest mice squeaked excitedly; they wanted teddy bears. Then all the mice went off to bed.

Mother Mouse put their blanket over them and tucked them in.

It wasn't a very big blanket and didn't quite cover them all.

Emmeline got most of the blanket because she was the oldest, then George, then Truffle. But the littlest mice got none. They lay there shivering in the cold.

So Truffle gave them his part of the blanket, but now he was cold.

“Darn,” said Truffle, as he stared out into the darkness. “I wish I’d asked for a blanket and not a hula hoop.” Suddenly he sat up. “I know, I’ll wait for Santa to tell him I’ve changed my mind.”

He crept out of bed and tiptoed to the
mousehole door.

There he waited and waited,
but Santa didn't come.
"I can't see here," grumbled Truffle.
"I'll go outside where I can see farther."

"I'd better take
something
to eat in case
I get hungry."

He packed an apple core,
a bread crust,
and half a peanut,
and off he went into
the night, dragging
his picnic behind him.

It was very cold.

As he waited for Santa Claus,
Truffle got hungry.
First he ate his
bread crust very slowly.

Then he ate his
apple core very, *very* slowly.

Finally he ate his peanut half
very, very, *very* slowly.

But still Santa
did not come.
Truffle stood up
and brushed off
his whiskers.

"I will go to that hill over there, where I can see Santa and Santa can see me," he said firmly and plodded off.

In the woods a fox barked and an owl hooted. A tabby cat pricked up her ears. Truffle was scared, but he trudged on and on.

The clouds covered the stars. It was very dark.

Truffle felt all alone and very tired. He sat down and tried to watch for Santa, but his eyes kept shutting.

Softly it started to snow. Truffle fell asleep.

"Now!" said the fox.
"Before the snow covers him."

"Now!" said the owl.
"Before the greedy fox gets him."

"Now!" said the tabby cat.
"Because I'm very, very hungry."

Then, just before the fox jumped,
and the owl swooped,
and the tabby cat pounced . . .

. . . there was a tinkling
and jingling of sleigh bells.

There was a rattling
and creaking of harnesses.

There was a pattering and shuffling
of hooves. But Truffle was sound asleep and
didn't notice a thing—

until a reindeer
snorted in his face
and woke him up.

"Eek!" squeaked Truffle.

"What's this?" said Santa.
"A poor little mouse."

Truffle shivered.

"Why aren't you in bed?" asked Santa.

"I came out here to find you,"
mumbled Truffle, still half asleep
and rather muddled.
"I wanted a hula hoop . . .
but we really need a blanket."

"Hmm," said Santa, "I think
it's time I took you home."
He tucked Truffle into
his pocket . . .

. . . and away they went.
Over the fox, the owl,
and the tabby cat.
Over the forest and hills.
Over the fields and bushes.

Finally they reached Truffle's home.

Truffle was asleep again—so sound asleep that he didn't even stir when Santa fished him out of his pocket and returned him to the mousehole.

Santa spotted a crumpled piece of paper on the ground.

He unfolded it carefully.

“Deer Santer,” it said in tiny mouse letters, “I wood lik a hoola hup, blankit, hulla hoop, blankit.”

“Aha!” said Santa.
“I see!”

Emmeline was the first to wake up
on Christmas morning. She
squealed loudly and woke up
George, Truffle, and the littlest mice.
They all squealed too, for not only
were they lying under the reddest,
warmest, coziest blanket they had
ever seen, they were lying on
the most beautiful bed
in the whole world.

And Emmeline had her nurse's uniform . . .

George had his chemistry set . . .

the littlest mice had their tiny teddies . . .

and Truffle had his hula hoop!

He smiled happily, and on his whiskers
still clung a little bit of red fluff
from the bottom of Santa's pocket.